First published in the United States 1990 by

Atomium Books Inc.
Suite 300
1013 Centre Road
Wilmington, DE 19805.

First edition published in French, by Editions Fleurus, Paris, 1988
under the title "Achille Karaboudil."
Text and illustrations copyright © Editions Fleurus, Paris 1988.
English translation copyright © Atomium Books 1990.

Printed and bound in Belgium by
Color Print Graphix, Antwerp.
First U.S. Edition
ISBN 1-56182-030-X
2 4 6 8 10 9 7 5 3 1

Cool Calvin

Story by Ann Rocard
English text adapted
by Peter Wood

Illustrations
by Françoise Rousset

atomium books

Cool Calvin Crocodile was the star of the Smallville zoo.
People came to look at him all the time.
Calvin had a huge swimming pool all to himself,
with a red and yellow sun umbrella and a springy diving-board.
Calvin loved to do tricks and show off for people.
When they clapped and laughed, Calvin felt so proud of himself.

"I'm such a cool crocodile,"
Calvin would say to himself.
"That's why the zoo director
invited me to live here."

Calvin was very happy at the zoo,
but he was also very proud
that he came from Africa.
He would daydream about when he lived there.
Calvin remembered how he used to crawl
out of the river to visit the village school.
He used to put his head through the open window
and listen to the lessons.
Then he'd pretend to take a bite
out of the teacher for lunch!
A big crocodile smile would spread
across Calvin's face as he dreamed.

Calvin was admiring his zoo pool one day
when he stopped short with a shock.
"Something important is missing," he thought.
"How can people know that I come from Africa?
I need some pictures and stories to show them."
Calvin decided to put on his best bow tie
and go downtown to a book store.

By the time Calvin was ready, it was nighttime.
The zoo gates were closed.
The zookeeper was home watching television,
so Calvin crawled out of his pool and slid over the zoo wall.
"Time for a city-safari," Calvin chuckled to himself.

He scurried through the dark streets of Smallville.
Soon he came to some big stores. They had huge windows.
Calvin looked sideways and saw a tall, green animal.
"Hi," he said. No one answered.
"Nice to meet you," he tried again. "I'm Cool Calvin."
There was still no answer. "Who is this?" he wondered.
Calvin put on his glasses to take a closer look.
"Oh," he said with pleasure. "It's me!
This window is like a mirror.
Hmmmmm, what a cool-looking crocodile! What a classy tie!"
And he stamped his feet and smiled at himself.

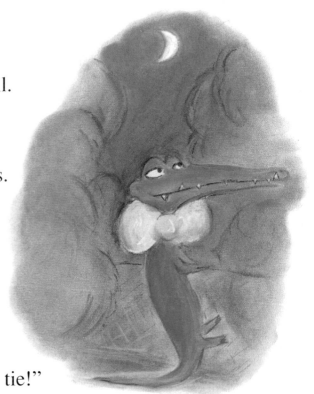

Soon it began to rain. Pit, pat. Then harder. Pitter-patter, pitter-patter.
A bolt of lightning lit up the dark sky.
"Zooks!" thought Calvin. "I need someplace dry."
He decided to stick his long, green tail into the road to stop a car.
"I'll ask the driver to take me to a book store.
Not only am I cool," he said to himself, "but I'm very clever."

Brrrrmmmm! Down the street roared a big, red car.
It just missed Calvin's tail.
"Eeeeeeeyikes," screamed the woman in the car.
"Did you see that big green monster? A crocodile!"
"You're nuts," said her husband. "A crocodile? In the street?"
"Go back and look!" she insisted.
They did. But there was no sign of a crocodile.

Calvin was hiding under a bridge, out of the rain and away from cars.
He looked around and saw someone else under the bridge.
A man was drawing a picture on the sidewalk with chalk.
Calvin walked over to look. "Hi, I'm Cool Calvin. What are you doing?"

"I'm an artist," said the man. "My name is Arthur.
I draw pictures on sidewalks.
If people like my pictures, they put money in my hat."

"I like your pictures," said Calvin. "But I have no money to put in your hat."

"That's all right," said Arthur. "You can give me a big smile instead."
So Calvin smiled a big crocodile smile.

"Maybe you can help me," said Calvin.
"I'm looking for a book store with pictures and stories about Africa."

"The stores are all closed until morning," said Arthur.
"Why not stay and sleep under the bridge with me?
You can share my sandwich for breakfast."

Calvin thought this was a good idea. He was already feeling hungry.

The next morning Arthur was busy drawing again.
Calvin got directions to the book store and said good-bye.

Soon Calvin came to a wide, busy street.
Cars and trucks were vrooming and honking.
"What terrible noise," he thought.
"I can hardly think with all this noise."
He looked around and saw an old woman carrying a big basket.
It was full of fruit and vegetables.
"I'll plug my ears with that green stuff," thought Calvin.
"It matches my skin."
He snatched two sprigs of parsley out of the basket
and stuffed them into his ears.
"Aaah!" he sighed. "That's better."

"Hey! Stop that thief!" shouted the old woman.
"He's stolen my parsley. I need it for my soup."

But Calvin didn't hear a word she said.
His ears were too full of parsley.
Calvin hurried across the busy street.
The old woman chased him, waving her umbrella angrily.

Soon Calvin came to the book store.
"Hi, I'm Cool Calvin," he said to the salesman.
"I want a book with pictures and stories about Africa
so I can show people where I come from."

"A-A-Africa?" said the man. "A-A-A b-b-book about Africa?"

"Yes. With pictures. I can read. I've been to school,"
said Calvin, feeling clever and cool.

"It's a p-p-pleasure to s-s-serve a c-c-crocodile.
We don't g-g-get m-m-many in here," said the frightened salesman.
"Here's a b-b-book about A-A-Africa."

It had a nice picture of a rhinoceros on the cover.
Calvin took the book, put the parsley back in his ears, and walked out of the shop.
The man seemed to be saying something, but Calvin couldn't hear him.

"Stop him! Stop him! He hasn't paid!" shouted the salesman.

Calvin strolled along the street.
Now both the old woman and the salesman were yelling and chasing after him.
But Calvin did not hear or see them.
Suddenly, WHOOPS! Calvin skidded and slipped along the sidewalk.
Three wide-eyed children were staring at him.
He had slipped right into their game of marbles.

"This looks like fun," said Calvin. "Can I try?"
The little girl told him how to play.
Calvin aimed carefully at the blue marble.
He was just about to try to hit it when . . .
the old woman and the salesman rounded the corner.

"There he is!" they shouted.

"Watch out!" warned the little boy with blond hair.
Calvin stretched himself and began to run.
"Hey, wait for us," called the children. "We want to play with you."

Cool Calvin ran down the street
chased by the old woman waving her umbrella,
the salesman, and the three children.

"Some safari!" thought Calvin.
"What can I do?
I'd better go back to the zoo."

He saw a policeman with a big, bristly moustache.
"Which way to the zoo?" called Calvin, trying to stay cool.

"Turn right, go straight ten blocks,
then turn left," said the policeman.
"But they won't let you in dressed up like that.
You're too early for Halloween."

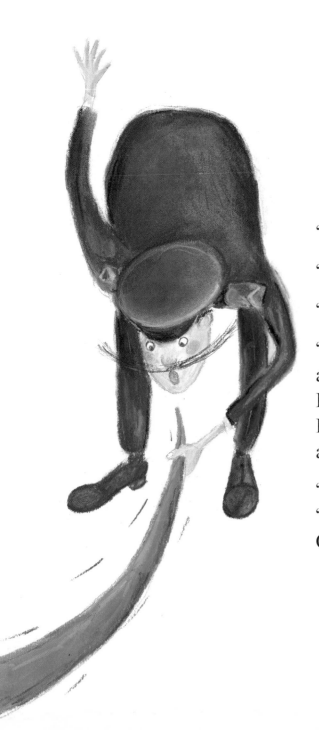

"What do you mean?" asked Calvin.

"Take off that mask," laughed the policeman.

"What mask?" asked Calvin, feeling very confused.

"That long, green tail doesn't fool me," said the policeman,
and he gave Calvin's tail a big, strong pull.
It didn't come off, of course.
Instead Calvin opened his jaws as wide as they could go
and howled.

"Eeeeeyipes! It's real," shouted the policeman.
"Help! An escaped crocodile!
Catch him! He's getting away . . ."

Calvin began to run as fast as he could, but now he was being chased
by the old lady . . . and the salesman . . . and the three children
. . . and the policeman with the big, bristly moustache.

"What can I do?" Calvin asked himself.
"I know! I'll take a taxi back to the zoo."

Just then a bright, yellow taxi came driving up the street.
The taxi was too small for Calvin to fit inside,
so he jumped on top of the taxi's roof and landed with a THUMP.

The taxi-driver was so frightened that he darted out the door and ran away.

Everyone else in the street started running too.
Everyone was frightened.

"Come back," called Calvin from the top of the taxi.
"I'm Cool Calvin, the star of the Smallville zoo.
Why is everyone running away from me?"

"I'm not running," said a voice.
"But I think you'd better get off the top of that taxi."
Calvin looked across the street and saw Arthur the artist.

"Come with me. I'll take you home to the zoo," called Arthur.
Calvin slid down the back of the taxi.

Arthur climbed onto Calvin's back and Calvin ran as fast as he could.
No one could catch them. Not the policeman with the big, bristly moustache.
Not the three children who wanted to play. Not the book store salesman.
And certainly not the little old lady waving her umbrella.

"Why is everyone chasing me?" Calvin asked Arthur.

"Everyone is chasing you because you did such silly things today," said Arthur.

"Silly things? But I'm a clever crocodile," said Calvin.
"I only wanted to get some pictures and stories about Africa."
Then Calvin began to cry — big crocodile tears.

"I didn't mean to make you sad," said Arthur.

"I'm sad that I did silly things," said Calvin.
"But I'm really crying because I lost my book about Africa!"

Calvin couldn't stop crying.
"Now I can't show people pictures of where I come from," he sobbed.

"Don't cry," said Arthur. "Don't you remember? I'm an artist.
I can draw pictures of Africa for you.
I'll visit you everyday and draw pictures around your pool."

Calvin stopped crying.
His unhappy face spread into a big, crocodile smile.

As the moon began to rise over the zoo, Cool Calvin gave Arthur a huge hug
and began dreaming of sidewalks filled with pictures of Africa.